I0610297

St. John's Parish

Daily Hymns

Thirty-Second Anniversary of Sunday Schools, St. John's Parish...

St. John's Parish

Daily Hymns
Thirty-Second Anniversary of Sunday Schools, St. John's Parish...

ISBN/EAN: 9783337089399

Printed in Europe, USA, Canada, Australia, Japan

Cover: Foto ©Andreas Hilbeck / pixelio.de

More available books at **www.hansebooks.com**

DAILY HYMNS.

THIRTY-SECOND

ANNIVERSARY OF SUNDAY SCHOOLS,

ST. JOHN'S PARISH, WATERBURY.

E. P. DUTTON AND COMPANY,
BOSTON: 135 WASHINGTON STREET.
NEW YORK: 762 BROADWAY.
1868.

Entered, according to Act of Congress, in the year 1867, by

E. P. DUTTON AND COMPANY,

In the Clerk's Office of the District Court for the District
of Massachusetts.

Daily Hymns.

——◆——

DAY of wrath, that day of burning,
　Seer and Sibyl speak concerning,
All the world to ashes turning.

Oh, what fear shall it engender,
When the Judge shall come in splendor,
Strict to mark, and just to render.

Trumpet scattering sounds of wonder,
Rending sepulchres asunder,
Shall resistless summons thunder.

All aghast then Death shall shiver,
And great Nature's frame shall quiver.
When the graves their dead deliver.

Book where actions are recorded,
All the ages have afforded
Shall be brought, and dooms awarded.

When shall sit the Judge unerring,
He 'll unfold all here occurring,
No just vengeance then deferring.

What shall I say, that time pending?
Ask what advocate's befriending,
When the just man needs defending.

Dreadful KING, all power possessing,
Saving freely those confessing,
Save Thou me, O Fount of Blessing!

Think, O JESUS, for what reason
Thou didst bear earth's spite and treason,
Nor me lose in that dread season!

Seeking me Thy worn feet hasted,
On the cross Thy soul death tasted:
Let such travail not be wasted!

Righteous Judge of retribution !
Make me gift of absolution,
Ere that day of execution !

Culprit-like I plead, heart-broken,
On my cheek Shame's crimson token ;
Let the pardoning words be spoken !

Thou who Mary gav'st remission,
Heard'st the dying thief's petition,
Cheer with hope my lost condition !

Though my prayers be void of merit,
What is needful Thou confer it,
Lest I endless fire inherit.

Be there, Lord, my place decided
With Thy sheep, from goats divided,
Kindly to Thy right hand guided.

When the accursed away are driven,
To eternal burnings given,
Call me with the blessed to Heaven !

I beseech Thee, prostrate lying,
Heart as ashes, contrite, sighing,
Care for me when I am dying!

Day of tears and late repentance,
Man shall rise to hear his sentence:
Him, the child of guilt and error,
Spare, LORD, in that hour of terror!

THOMAS OF CELANO.

FORTH from the dark and stormy sky,
  Lord, to Thine altar's shade we fly:
Forth from the world, its doubt and fear,
Saviour, we seek Thy refuge here :
Weary and weak, Thy grace we pray —
Turn not, O Lord, Thy guests away !

Long have we roamed in want and pain ;
Long have we sought Thy rest in vain:
Wildered in doubt, in darkness lost,
Long have our souls been tempest-tost:
Low at Thy feet our sins we lay —
Turn not, O Lord, Thy guests away !

BISHOP HEBER.

FRIDAY AFTER ASH-WEDNESDAY.

LORD, many times I am aweary quite
  Of mine own self, my sin, my vanity —
Yet be not Thou, or I am lost outright,
    Weary of me.

And hate against myself I often bear,
  And enter with myself in fierce debate :
Take Thou my part against myself, nor share
    In that just hate !

Best friends might loathe us, if what things
    perverse
We know of our own selves, they also knew.
Lord, Holy One ! if Thou who knowest worse
    Shouldst loathe us too !

R. C. TRENCH.

FAITH calmeth every care —
 O heart, be still!
There falls no single hair
 Without God's will.
Even here the Lord bestows
 'Mid toil His rest;
And soon will come repose,
 Where *all* is blest.

Faith drieth every tear —
 O look above!
Commit to Him each fear
 Whose name is Love.
He knows what needful is,
 His ways are just;
All, all the care is His,
 And thine the trust.

Faith nerves the trembling soul
　　With strength serene;
High o'er the waves that roll,
　　Its star is seen.
O heart! that star hath shone
　　In life's dark days:
In death it shineth on,
　　With Heaven's own rays.

Faith has its triumph song
　　In grief and care —
The night will not be long;
　　The morn, how fair!
O Faith! thy very tears
　　Are jewels bright:
How soon shall endless years
　　Crown thee as Sight!

　　　　　　　　F. Hiller.

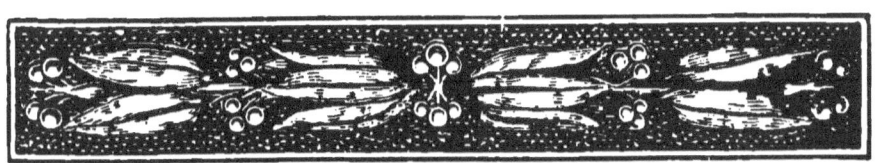

FIRST SUNDAY IN LENT.

LORD, I must walk *with* Thee,
  Not follow distantly.
Only Thine arm can raise,
Only Thy loving gaze
Bid earthly hopes depart,
And fill my longing heart.

Therefore not only say,
" Arise, and come away ! "
But come Thou to my side,
Embrace, and onward guide ;
And, as life's trials press,
Help Thou my helplessness.

Saviour, I will not grieve
For Thee my all to leave.
Thou whisperest pleadingly,
" Do it for love of Me ! "

Looking up in Thine eyes,
How light the sacrifice!

What things I prized before
I, one by one, give o'er; .
All that my life could bless,
Earth's love, earth's happiness.
Lord, do not Thou forsake —
Then, then my heart would break!

No, Thou dost these recall
Only to give me all, —
All that is hid in Thee, —
Thy love, Thy sympathy.
My Saviour, at Thy side
My soul is satisfied!

Close to Thee would I cling,
Closer in suffering.
Heavy may be the night,
In Thee I find my light.
The way I cannot see —
I care not, 't is with Thee.

Though life's dark clouds may hide
Earth's pleasure and its pride,
What matters it to me?
So that they hide not Thee.
Let yon poor stars decline,
If the full Sun but shine.

Only for this I pray, —
Turn not Thy face away!
Let me but hear Thy voice,
And love, if not rejoice!
Then darkness shall be light,
Then faith shall turn to sight;
Till, safe at home, my heart
Shall know Thee as Thou art.

SORROW now the harp is stringing
  For the everlasting singing,
    Teaching us to soar above ;
Where the blessed choir, palm-bearing,
Harps are playing, crowns are wearing,
    Round the Throne with songs of love.

Sorrow makes our faith abiding,
Lowly, childlike, and confiding ;
    Sorrow, who can speak thy grace !
Though on earth called tribulation,
Heaven has nobler appellation :
    Not thus honored all our race.

Though the healthful powers were willing,
All the Master's will fulfilling,
    By obedience to be tried ;
Yet 't is still no less a blessing,
Such a Master's care possessing,
    In His furnace to abide.

In the depth of keenest anguish,
More and more the heart will languish
   After Jesus' loving heart.
For one blessing only crying —
Make me like Thee in Thy dying,
   Then Thy endless life impart!

Till at length, with sighs all breaking,
Through each bond its passage taking,
   Lo, the veil is rent in twain!
Who remembers now life's sorrow?
Cloudless shines that bright To-morrow
   Over earth's long night of pain.

                          HARTMANN.

TUESDAY.

O LORD, my heart's chief treasure!
    That heart Thou wilt ∙not leave.
With Thee even pain is pleasure,
    Without Thee joy would grieve.
Heaven has no bliss to win me
    Save what it draws from Thee;
Come, Lord, and dwell within me!
    Then life a heaven shall be.

Bring all that fancy offers,
    Or poet's heart could paint;
Wealth in its golden coffers,
    Love without sorrow's taint;
How poor, how weak their blessing
    When Thou art known aright!
Shall we, the Sun possessing,
    Turn to the stars for light?

Sunshine in life's dark hours,
    Fount in its desert ways,

Refuge when tempest lowers,
  Hope in its dreary days!
Such art Thou, Lord, in sadness,
  And oh, in joy how bright!
The very Life of gladness,
  The very Light of light.

The waste a garden seemeth
  Beneath Thy loving eyes;
Thy smile in darkness beameth,
  And thousand stars arise.
O guide me as Thou willest!
  Through waters calm or wild;
Thy voice the tempest stilleth,
  Thy hand shall lead Thy child.

Since naught from Thee can sever,
  Then take which way is best;
Only be with me ever,
  In battle as in rest.
Then sorrow shall not grieve me,
  And pain be all forgot;
My Lord, I will not leave Thee:
  O Jesus, leave me not!

F. MEYER.

MATINS.

GOD of the morning! we bow at Thine
altar,
Low at Thy footstool for mercy we kneel.
Why should our steps at Thy temple-gate
falter?
Here Thou hast promised Thy love to re-
veal.

God of the morning! this sweet, sunlit quiet
Calms us to conquer the toils of the day:
Wild in the world human passions run riot;
Guide Thou our steps in Thy heavenward
way!

God of the morning! to shield from temptation,
Bid us remember the spells of the place:

There, at yon Font, spake our life's dedication;
There, at yon altar, we knelt for Thy grace.

God of the morning! the love that has kept
    us,
On through life's journey forever shall keep.
Sunshine may fail, but Thy light shall be left
    us;
  While Thou art smiling Thy child cannot
    weep.

God of the morning! to labor returning,
  Now we would carry Thy blessing away:
Oh, be Thy love on our heart's altar burning;
  Oh, be Thy presence our comfort and stay!

God of the morning! Thy sunshine is stream-
    ing
Far over earth with its care and its strife;
So may Thy love in its purity beaming,
  Light up the by-ways and shadows of life!

A. G. R.

THURSDAY.

EVENSONG.

DAY'S weary work is done,
　　Our spirits yearn for rest;
Surely yon golden sun
　　Is in his setting blest.
He sinks in Heaven's light,
　　We in earth-darkness pine;
Oh, rise upon our night,
　　　　Saviour divine!

Soft as a voice from Heaven
　　The bells of evening peal;
Has there no balm been given,
　　These earthly woes to heal?
Yon cross-crowned tower smiles
　　Through the sweet twilight air;
Enter those sacred aisles,
　　　　And kneel in prayer.

The world's rude strife and din
  Back from this Temple flee;
There 's Heaven's own rest within,
  And Heaven's serenity.
The anthem's solemn tone
  Peals grandly on the ear; —
Alone, yet not alone,
    For God is here.

Thou who canst give the peace
  Which earth takes not away,
Bid all the sorrows cease
  That cloud life's little day!
Thy light and truth fail never,
  Though we in darkness range;
Our hearts are changing ever,
    Thine cannot change.

Oh, let this quiet hour,
  This sacred, sunset rest,
This silent church have power
  To calm the fevered breast!

Out from the world we come
To Thee, at close of day.
Meet us in this Thy home, —
Bless us alway!

A. G. R.

I WAS wandering and weary,
   When my Saviour came unto me;
For the ways of sin grew dreary,
   And the world had ceased to woo me:
And I thought I heard Him say,
As He came along His way.
      O silly souls! come near Me;
      My sheep should never fear Me;
      I am the Shepherd true.

At first I would not hearken,
   And put off till the morrow;
But life began to darken,
   And I was sick with sorrow:
And I thought I heard Him say,
As He came along His way,

O silly souls! come near Me;
My sheep should never fear Me;
I am the Shepherd true.

At last I stopped to listen,
　His voice could not deceive me;
I saw His kind eyes glisten,
　So anxious to relieve me:
And I thought I heard Him say,
As He came along His way,
　　　O silly souls! come near Me;
　　　My sheep should never fear Me;
　　　I am the Shepherd true.

He took me on His shoulder,
　And tenderly He kissed me;
He bade my love be bolder,
　And said how He had missed me:
And I'm sure I heard him say,
As He went along His way,
　　　O silly souls! come near Me;
　　　My sheep should never fear Me;
　　　I am the Shepherd true.

Strange gladness seemed to move Him,
  Whenever I did better;
And He coaxed me so to love Him,
  As if He were my debtor:
And I always heard Him say,
As He went along His way,
     O silly souls! come near Me;
     My sheep should never fear Me;
     I am the Shepherd true.

I thought His love would weaken
  As more and more He knew me;
But it burneth like a beacon,
  And its light and heat go through me.
And I ever hear Him say,
As He goes along His way,
     O silly souls! come near Me;
     My sheep should never fear Me;
     I am the Shepherd true.

Let us do then, dearest brothers,
  What will best and longest please us;
Follow not the ways of others,
  But trust ourselves to Jesus:

We shall ever hear Him say,
As He goes along His way,
  O silly souls! come near Me;
  My sheep should never fear Me;
  I am the Shepherd true.

F. W. FABER.

MY God, I thank Thee, who hast made
    The earth so bright;
So full of splendor and of joy,
    Beauty and light;
So many glorious things are here,
    Noble and right!

I thank Thee, too, that Thou hast made
    Joy to abound;
So many gentle thoughts and deeds
    Circling us round,
That in the darkest spot of earth
    Some love is found.

I thank Thee *more* that all our joy
    Is touched with pain;
That shadows fall on brightest hours;
    That thorns remain;
So that earth's bliss may be our guide,
    And not our chain.

For 'Thou who knowest, Lord, how soon
    Our weak heart clings,
Hast given us joys, tender and true,
    Yet all with wings,
So that we see, gleaming on high,
    Diviner things!

I thank Thee, Lord, that Thou hast kept
    The best in store.
We have enough, yet not too much
    To long for more :
A yearning for a deeper peace,
    Not known before.

I thank Thee, Lord, that here our souls,
    Though amply blest,
Can never find, although they seek,
    A perfect rest, —
Nor ever shall, until they lean
    On Jesus' breast!

                    A. A. PROCTOR.

SECOND SUNDAY IN LENT.

GOD knows the best!
  His love can make life's darkness clear,
Chase the heart's winter from the breast,
  And send a summer all the year.
The souls who yield to Him are blest
  With foretastes of their heavenly cheer;
And earthly strife or earthly rest
  It matters not when Home is near.

    God knows the way!
  Trust Him to lead thy steps aright.
Oh let the path be what it may,
  'T is smooth to faith, though rough to sight!
Seek not earth's sunshine, nor delay
  By pastures green and waters bright;
For earthly night or earthly day
  It matters little in His light.

God knows the end!
His is the Land of love divine:
Thither thy journey all shall tend
  Through storms that beat, or suns that shine.
He shall from every ill defend,
  Though all against thy soul combine;
And earthly foe or earthly friend
  It matters not, if He is thine!

A. G. R.

WHO to the end endures,
  Through earthly lures,
Through the world's fight and frown,
  Shall win the crown.
But oh! what hours of pain,
  What struggles vain,
What foes, what trials great
  His heart await!
Faith on life's battle-field
  Must never yield!

There 's many a weary night
  In that fierce fight;
And the strength may not fail,
  Nor the heart quail, —
For dauntless faith must dare
  Death and despair.
But, O my God! Thine own
  Are not alone:
Thou comest in the strife, —
  The Life of life!

Then courage, brothers, come !
  Yonder 's our home, —
Beyond the battle's heat,
  Serene and sweet.
Lay not our weapons down :
  First Cross, then Crown !
By the brave heart and hand
  The Lord doth stand ;
And death with Him shall be
  A victory !

O Lord ! my weakness lies
  Before Thine eyes.
Let Thy strong, loving arm
  Shield me from harm !
That arm my strength shall be ;
  Fight Thou for me !
I am but helpless dust ;
  Thy might I trust !
Triumph and rest are Thine —
  O make them mine !

F. HILLER.

THIS did not once so trouble me,
    That better I could not love Thee;
        But now I feel and know
That only when we love, we find
How far our hearts remain behind
        The love they should bestow.

When we had little care to call
On Thee, and scarcely prayed at all,
        We seemed enough to pray:
But now we only think with shame,
How seldom to Thy glorious Name
        Our lips their offerings pay.

And when we gave yet slighter heed
Unto our brother's suffering need,
        Our hearts reproached us then
Not half so much as now, that we
With such a careless eye can see
        The wants and woes of men.

In doing is this knowledge won,
To see what yet remains undone:
   With this our pride repress —
And give us grace, a growing store,
That day by day we may do more,
   And may esteem it less.

R. C. TRENCH.

WEDNESDAY.

LORD, 't is a weary night —
I long for life and light!
Dark clouds are in the sky,   .
The winds are rising high,
And o'er my troubled soul
Waves of temptation roll.

But oh, one smile of Thine
Like thousand suns would shine!
One little look of love
My wilful heart would move;
One breath to flame would bring
The faith so languishing.

Black clouds of sin confound,
And devils gather round,
And all life's weariness
Weighs down with sore distress,
And the bright realms of day
Seem years and years away.

3

O Lord, Thy strength impart !
Give me a better heart, —
More thankful for Thy light,
More patient through the night,
More apt Thy praise to sing,
Less weak and wavering.

Lord, I am nought but sin,
Evil without, within.
Oh can it truly be
That Thou dost care for me;
That, in Thy goodness blest,
I on Thy heart may rest?

If but that rest is mine,
If Thou wilt call me Thine,
Then night may frown above,
I will but see Thy love ;
Its storms may thunder near,
Thy voice alone I 'll hear.

Its blasts shall seem but gales
From Heaven's peaceful vales ;
Its frost shall change to balm,

Its fever sink to calm.
Lord, from Thy loving eyes
My sun of life shall rise!

Forgive this faithless mind,
So thankless and so blind!
Thou hast not left my side,
Even here Thy love doth guide;
And, though I cannot see,
I feel Thy grace with me.

This night will brighten soon;
Life has its cloudless noon,
Its islands of repose
From weariness and woes, —
And Thou wilt lead me there,
In sunshine fresh and fair.

Looking back on the way,
My grateful heart shall say,
Mercy and truth, O Lord,
In all Thy paths accord!
The warmth Thy love can bring,
Turns Winter into Spring.

Thus even in my prayer
Faith breathes a purer air;
The song, in tears begun,
Now into smiles hath run.
But smiles and tears both say,
Be with me, Lord, alway!

A. G. R.

THURSDAY.

MAKE use of me, my God!
  Let me not be forgot;
A broken vessel cast aside,
  One whom Thou needest not.

I am Thy creature, Lord,
  And made by hands divine;
And I am part, however mean,
  Of this great world of Thine.

Thou usest all Thy works,
  The weakest things that be;
Each has a service of its own,
  For all things wait on Thee.

Thou usest the high stars,
  The tiny drops of dew,
The giant peak and little hill; —
  My God, oh use me too!

Thou usest tree and flower,
  The rivers vast and small;
The eagle great, the little bird
  That sings upon the wall.

Thou usest the wide sea,
  The little hidden lake;
The pine upon the Alpine cliff,
  The lily in the brake;

The huge rock in the vale,
  The sand-grain by the sea;
The thunder of the rolling cloud,
  The murmur of the bee.

All things do serve Thee here,
  All creatures, great and small;
Make use of me, of me, my God,
  The meanest of them all!

H. BONAR.

THOU deep abyss of blessed Love,
   In Jesus Christ to us unsealed!
Fire which no finite heart could prove,
   Depths to no human thought revealed;
Thou lovest sinners — lovest me,
Thou blessest those who cursèd Thee.
O great, O kind, O loving One,
What worthless creatures shin'st Thou on!

Thou King of Light! our deepest longing
   Is shallow to Thy depths of grace;
Deep are the woes to us belonging,
   But deeper far Thy joy to bless.
Teach us to trust the Father's love,
Still looking to the Son above.
Blest Spirit! through our spirits pour
True prayers and praises evermore.

ZINZENDORF.

SATURDAY.

OVER the waves of life's troublesome sea
  Jesus still walks while the loud billows
    roar ;
And to the haven where fain it would be,
  Bringeth Faith's ship from the far-distant
    shore.
Night cannot hide Him, and storms cannot
    sever :
Whom the Lord loveth He loveth forever.

Hearts that are weary, and eyes that are dim,
  Look unto Christ the Consoler, and rest !
Tempest and cloud turn to sunshine with Him ;
  Grief hath its gladness, and mourning is
    blest.
Cast on the Lord all thy burden of sorrow :
Weeping to-night bringeth joy on the morrow.

Therefore rejoice when the wild ocean rolls!
  Life knows no storm where the Lord can-
    not save.
Still in your patience possess ye your souls;
  God, as of old, is in whirlwind and wave.
He who with Jesus would triumph in gladness,
First must have wept with the Saviour in
    sadness.

Soon will the morning rise fadeless and fair;
  Soon will the toils of the voyagers cease.
Crystal and calm is the sea flowing there, —
  All of life's tumult is hushed into peace.
Thither, O Lord! guide me over the billow;
And in the storm let Thy breast be my pillow!

EDELING.

THIRD SUNDAY IN LENT.

I AM in danger, —
  Be Thou my defence!
Pain and temptation
  Banish from hence!
Guard and protect me,
  By night and by day;
Guide through the wilderness!
  Light on my way!

I am in danger:
  The world, with its cares,
Digs for me pitfalls,
  Sets for me snares.
Careless my footsteps,
  Ready to roam:
How shall I ever
  Come safe to my home?

I am in danger, —
  Afflictions are near ;
Hope droops her pinions,
  Faith shrinks to fear.
Shall I make shipwreck
  Of love and of trust ?
Be Thou my refuge !
  I am but dust.

I am in danger :
  Each hour as it flies
Seeks to decoy me
  Away from the skies.
Wave-beaten sea-sand,
  Wind-smitten reed, —
Such is my weakness,
  Help Thou my need.

I am in danger :
  Death's dreary vale
Stretches before me,
  Shall I not quail ?
Can I encounter
  The gloom of its night ?

Star of the wanderer,
　Be Thou my light!

I am in danger, —
　Yet says Thy voice,
"Doubt not, and tremble not;
　Trust and rejoice."
Then, kind and mighty One!
　Then shall I be
Never in danger, —
　Ever with Thee!

MONDAY.

JESUS! the very thought is sweet!
In that dear name all heart-joys meet:
But oh! than honey sweeter far
The glimpses of His presence are.

No word is sung more sweet than this;
No sound is heard more full of bliss;
No thought brings sweeter comfort nigh
Than Jesus, Son of God most high.

Jesus, the hope of souls forlorn,
How good to them for sin that mourn!
To them that seek Thee, oh how kind!
But what art Thou to them that find!

No tongue of mortal can express,
No pen can write the blessedness,
He only who hath proved it knows
What bliss from love of Jesus flows.

O Jesus! King of wondrous might!
O victor, glorious from the fight!
Sweetness that cannot be expressed,
And altogether loveliest!

Abide with us, O Lord, to-day,
Fulfil us with Thy grace we pray;
And with Thine own true sweetness feed
Our souls, from sin and darkness freed.

St. Bernard.

TUESDAY.

I THANK Thee for the loneliness
  That brings me near to Thee; —
Thanks that no other heart can bless,
  No other eye can see!
I never knew the depth, the height,
  Of heavenly love before:
O Lord! Thy presence gilds my night,
  It brightens more and more.

What matter, in that lucid gleam,
  If stars grow bright or pale?
Shall we of lesser glories dream
  Who look within the veil?
Why count the little earthly loss,
  When gifts from Heaven flow down?
Lord, Thou for me hast set the Cross
  With jewels of the Crown.

A. G. R.

A RT thou weary? art thou languid?
  Art thou sore distrest?
"Come to Me," saith One, "and coming
    Be at rest."

Hath He marks to lead me to Him,
  If He be my guide?
"In His hands and feet are wound-prints,
    And His side."

Is there diadem, as monarch,
  That His brow adorns?
"Yes, a crown in very surety, —
    But of Thorns!"

If I find Him, if I follow,
  What His guerdon here?
"Many a sorrow, many a labor,
    Many a tear."

If I still hold closely to Him,
  What hath He at last?
" Sorrow vanquished, labor ended,
  Jordan past."

If I ask Him to receive me,
  Will He say me nay?
" Not till earth and not till heaven
  Pass away."

Finding, following, keeping, struggling,
  Is He sure to bless?
" Angels, martyrs, prophets, virgins,
  Answer Yes!"

St. Stephen the Sabite.

4

THURSDAY.

FROM Thee, O Lord, I take my lot!
    Sunshine or shade, it matters not:
For Thou canst make earth's shadows shine
With radiance lovely and divine.

O doubting heart! be strong and brave!
Hath not the Saviour power to save?
His is no empty, mocking name;
When did He put thy trust to shame?

Oh, many a night upon my way
Thy starlight shone as bright as day.
I wept for threatening clouds of woes —
Lo! while I wept the morning rose.

Often I saw no help, no hope;
Unarmed with furious foes to cope.
Then unto Thee I raised my cry, —
"Save, or I perish!" Thou wert nigh.

I saw Thy fiery chariots stand;
I saw the hosts at Thy right hand, —
Angels and ministers of grace,
To aid the souls that seek Thy face.

Yes, Lord! Thine hour comes always sure:
Though weeping may a night endure,
Joy stealeth down, through paths forlorn,
And draws the curtains of the dawn.

" Faithful and true " Thy heavenly name;
Thine earthly child repeats the same, —
Faithful and true, in smiles or tears,
Thy ways to me through life's long years.

There came no storm without its calm, —
No grief without its healing balm:
All shadows were by sunshine cast;
They fled, but sunshine yet doth last.

Therefore I always will rejoice,
By day or night, to hear Thy voice, —
" O doubting heart! why troubled be?
I am the Lord; believe on Me! "

LAVATER.

FRIDAY.

I HAVE had my happy days,
  Followed life through pleasant ways,
    Joys unnumbered bloomed in all:
Now with patient faith I go
Through the desert walks of woe —
    In each life some tears must fall!

Lord, my sin is in Thy sight,
And Thy strokes are far more light
    Than the load of guilt I bear:
Then shall I, a sinner, shrink
Sorrow's bitter cup to drink?
    Heaven mixes sweetness there.

Unto Thee I give my heart;
Life and love may all depart:
    Lord, I love Thee more than life!

Earthly refuge turns to dust;
Thou my Refuge art, my Trust:
    I shall conquer in the strife!

Death may come, but death shall be
Messenger of life to me:
    Can I grieve to see him near?
In the dark and shadowy vale
Thou, my Saviour, wilt not fail —
    And with Thee I feel no fear.

I will take, in patient faith,
Sorrow, darkness, pain, and death,
    Looking only unto Thee:
Lord, I yield me to Thy will!
Be it blessing, be it ill,
    All shall work for good to me.

GELLERT.

SATURDAY.

TIME flows on with me
　　To Eternity!
Morning fades to evening light;
Weeks roll quickly out of sight:
　Happy he whose day
　Stainless steals away!

　Shifting hopes and fears
　Mark the changeful years.
Where are now the hours gay,
Where the griefs of yesterday?
　Smiles and tears are one,
　When the night is done.

　Though the world may seem
　Shadowy as a dream,
Yet Thy promise, Lord, is sure;
And Thy truth shall still endure.
　Stars may pale and fall —
　Heaven still beams o'er all!

While to Thee I cling,
Time can only bring
Light and joy and sunshine's gleam,
Heaven's truth in earthly dream:
Even tears shall be
Rainbow drops to me.

Happy, happy lot!
Thou who changest not
Rulest all my changeful days, —
And thus ever to Thy praise,
Time flows on with me
To Eternity!

KARL GARVE.

FOURTH SUNDAY IN LENT.

LORD of mercy and of might!
Of mankind the life and light!
Maker, teacher infinite!
    Jesus, hear and save!

Who, when Sin's tremendous doom
Gave creation to the tomb,
Did not scorn the Virgin's womb, —
    Jesus, hear and save!

Mighty monarch, Saviour mild,
Humbled to a little child,
Captive, beaten, bound, reviled, —
    Jesus, hear and save!

Throned above celestial things,
Borne aloft on angels' wings,
Lord of lords and King of kings!
    Jesus, hear and save!

Who shall yet return from high,
Robed in light and majesty,
Hear us! help us when we cry!
    Jesus, hear and save!

BISHOP HEBER.

MONDAY.

STILL waters, pastures green,
  Such, Lord, these years have been.
Such flowers have bloomed for me,
Such fountains flowed from Thee,
That even life's desert ways
Shall echo to Thy praise.

Still Memory's loveliest light
Lingers around the night
When first beneath Thy cross
I felt the world but dross,
And gained the Pearl of Price
In my poor sacrifice.

O Holy One! I came
To Thee in sin and shame:
I found the welcome free,
The ring, the feast for me;
The robe of righteousness, —
All that my soul could bless!

Freely Thy love bestowed :
I reap not what I sowed.
No ! were Thy heart like mine,
The floods of wrath divine
Had poured, in vengeance dread,
Over my guilty head.

But mercy, love, and grace
Opened me their embrace.
The wanderer found a fold ;
The needy, wealth untold ;
The sinner sank to rest
Upon a Saviour's breast.

O Lord, what words can tell
That bliss unspeakable !
What song by angels sung,
What seraph's burning tongue,
Could utter half the praise
My soul to Thee should raise.

Low at Thy cross I fall ;
Thou hast my life, my all.
I breathe no other prayer,

I have no other care,
But to abide in Thee,
And Thy salvation see.

Lead me as Thou hast led;
Feed with the living Bread!
Let Sorrow do its worst,
I hunger not, nor thirst,
For 'neath the desert skies
The heavenly manna lies.

Still waters, pastures green,
Everywhere calm, serene;
Wild wastes and dreary sands
Turned into pleasant lands:
Such are Thy paths of peace;
Such, until life shall cease.

Therefore I follow on —
The night is almost gone.
Death's river flows afar,
Lit by the Morning Star.
Oh let its billows be
Still waters unto me!

TUESDAY.

I COME to Thee once more, my God!
  No longer will I roam;
For I have sought the wide world through,
  And never found a home.

Though bright and many are the spots
  Where I have built a nest,
Yet in the brightest still I pined
  For more abiding rest.

Riches could bring me joy and power,
  And they were fair to see;
Yet gold was but a sorry god
  To serve instead of Thee.

Then honor and the world's good word
  Appeared a nobler faith;
Yet could I rest on bliss that hung
  And trembled on a breath?

The pleasure of the passing hour
  My spirit next could wile;
But soon, full soon, my heart fell sick
  Of pleasure's weary smile.

More selfish grown, I worshipped health,
  The flush of manhood's power;
But then it came and went so quick,
  It was but for an hour.

And thus a not unkindly world
  Hath done its best for me;
Yet I have found, O God! no rest,
  No harbor short of Thee.

For Thou hast made this wondrous soul
  All for Thyself alone:
Ah, send Thy sweet, transforming grace
  To make it more Thine own.

F. W. Faber.

WEDNESDAY.

AROUND and within us the night-shadows
    close —
Oh where, save in Thee, can our spirits re-
    pose?
Thy light through the darkness our beacon
    shall be —
Thou Rest of the Weary! we come unto Thee!

Life's burdens are heavy, they weigh on our
    breast;
But Thou, the Consoler, hast promised us
    rest.
The sadder our hearts are the kinder Thou 'lt
    be —
Dear Rest of the Weary! we come unto Thee.

What billows shall fright us if Thou art but
    near?
With Thee what protection! without Thee what
    fear!

O Hope of the Sinner! shine, beckon to me!
For, Rest of the Weary! we come unto Thee.

So frail, so uncertain our joy and our woe,
What day shall bring either we never can
      know:
Thou only our Refuge unchanging canst be;
O Rest of the Weary! we come unto Thee.

Our sunshine hath shadows; smiles tremble
      to tears;
Dark days will steal into the brightest of
      years.
Too restless our joys are; too ready to flee:
Thou Rest of the Weary! we come unto Thee

Dear Star of our morning, and Moon of our
      night!
Our darkness before Thee soon dawns into
      light.
How calm must life's current flow on to the
      sea,
When, Rest of the Weary! we come unto
      Thee.

Each day, every hour, Thy children would
   come ;
Each day, every hour, speeds nearer our Home.
How fast earth's fair hopes to forgetfulness
   flee !
But, Rest of the Weary ! we come unto Thee.

When o'er life's wild ocean the last sunset
   glows,
And tired hearts yearn for a dreamless repose,
Then, over the waves of Eternity's sea,
O Rest of the Weary ! we come unto Thee.

A. G. R.

5

THURSDAY.

O GOD! my sins are manifold; against my life they cry,
And all my guilty deeds foregone up to Thy temple fly:
Wilt Thou release my trembling soul, that to despair is driven?
"Forgive!" a blessed voice replied, "and thou shalt be forgiven."

My foemen, Lord, are fierce and fell — they spurn me in their pride,
They render evil for my good, my patience they deride:
Arise, O King! and be the proud to righteous ruin driven, —
"Forgive!" an awful answer came, "as thou wouldst be forgiven."

Seven times, O Lord! I pardoned them;
 seven times they sinned again;
They practise still to work me woe, they triumph in my pain:
But let them dread my vengeance now, to
 just resentment driven.—
"Forgive!" the voice of thunder spake, "or
 never be forgiven!"

BISHOP HEBER.

FRIDAY.

MY God, I love Thee! not because
    I hope for Heaven thereby;
Nor because they who love Thee not
    Must burn eternally.

But O my Jesus! Thou didst me
    Upon the cross embrace; —
For me didst bear the nail and spear,
    And manifold disgrace;

And griefs and torments numberless,
    And sweat of agony, —
E'en death itself, — and all for one
    Who was Thine enemy!

Then why, O blessed Jesus Christ!
    Shall I not love Thee well?
Not for the sake of winning heaven,
    Nor of escaping hell, —

Not with the hope of gaining aught,
  Not seeking a reward,
But as Thyself hast lovèd me,
  O ever-loving Lord!

Even so I love Thee, and will love,
  And to Thy praise will sing,
Solely because Thou art my God,
  And my eternal King.

XAVIER.

SATURDAY.

O LORD! I grasp Thy hand,
　　As onward through the night
I journey to the land
　　Of everlasting light.
How safe that hand has led
　　Through years of mortal ill!
Sorrow and joy alike have fled;
　　But Thou art with me still.

Oh wondrous, wondrous were
　　The paths where Thou didst guide!
Rainbows and storms commingled there,
　　But Thou wert by my side.
It was the Lord's highway,
　　The way of holiness;
And whether bright or dark the day,
　　It only rose to bless.

Now that the midnight's gloom
　　Stealthily creepeth near;

Sepulchral shadows from the tomb
  With all their solemn fear, —
O Lord, my helper be,
  Though hidden from my sight!
Thy hand upholds as steadfastly
  In darkness as in light.

Then nerve my sinking faith :
  O take my hand in Thine!
Thy love is stronger far than death ;
  And, Lord, that love is mine.
It is but one black wave,
  And then a crystal sea ;
One dream of darkness in the grave,
  The morn, — Eternity!

Yes, though Love weep its tears,
  And Hope may scarce endure,
Steadily onward move the years, —
  Our endless home is sure.
A home, O Lord, with Thee!
  A home in Thy embrace —
Where Faith that followed trustingly
  Shall see Thee, face to face.

LIEBICH.

FIFTH SUNDAY IN LENT.

I BORE with thee long weary days and
    nights,
  Through many pangs of heart, through many
    tears ;
I bore with thee, thy hardness, coldness, slights,
  For three and thirty years.

Who else had dared for thee what I have
    dared ?
  I plunged the depth most deep from bliss
    above ;
I not My flesh, I not My spirit spared :
  Give thou Me love for love.

For thee I thirsted in the daily drought,
  For thee I trembled in the nightly frost :
Much sweeter thou than honey to My mouth,
  Why wilt thou still be lost ?

I bore thee on My shoulders and rejoiced;
  Men only marked upon My shoulders borne
The branding cross; and shouted hungry
    voiced,
  Or wagged their heads in scorn.

Thee did nails grave upon My hands; thy
    name
  Did thorns for frontlets stamp between Mine
    eyes:
I, Holy One, put on thy guilt and shame, —
  I, God, Priest, Sacrifice.

A thief upon My right hand and My left;
  Six hours alone, athirst, in misery:
At length in death one smote My heart, and
    cleft
  A hiding-place for thee.

Nailed to the racking cross, than bed of down
  More dear, whereon to stretch Myself and
    sleep:
So did I win a kingdom, — share My crown;
  A harvest, — come and reap.

C. G. ROSSETTI.

MONDAY.

I WILL love Thee, O my Strength!
    Thou my only true Delight!
Till life's little day at length
    Shall be lost in Death's dark night.
Then my breaking heart shall be
Stayed for evermore on Thee.

I will love Thee, O my Life!
    Friend above all others dear!
For in sunshine or in strife
    Thou art ever, ever near.
And Thou, Lamb of God! Thy love
On the bitter cross didst prove.

Ah, that I so late have known
    All the blessedness in Thee!
How much peace and joy had flown
    Through these long years down to me!
Lord, I mourn my sinful fate,
That I love, alas! so late.

Yet I thank Thee, Heavenly Sun!
   That Thy life-restoring beams
Upon me have shone, and won
   My sad heart from troubled dreams.
In the darkness of my night
Thou hast said, " Let there be light!"

Give my eyes soft, cooling tears;
   Fill my soul with heavenly fire;
Let me love Thee, endless years,
   With an ever fresh desire;
May my soul and mind and heart
Never from Thy love depart.

I will love Thee, O my Crown!
   Though I bend beneath Thy rod:
Thou wilt smile though life may frown,
   Thou my changeless Lord and God.
And my grateful heart shall be
Thine to all eternity.

                    ANGELUS SILESIUS.

TUESDAY.

WAIT till the morning comes,
    Wait till the heavenly Homes
Open at His command
Who guides thee by the hand.
There, at the golden gates,
His crown, His welcome waits.

Thy cross, for His dear sake,
A little longer take.
For many weary years
He bore earth's toil and tears;
But oh how tenderly
Through life He leadeth thee!

His arm to lean upon,
His rest when work is done,
His smile to light thy way,
His blessing for thy stay, —

With these canst thou not bear
Thy little load of care?

What though some flowers fade,
What though some heavy shade
Makes all the future dim:
Lift up thine eyes to Him!
Shadows and earthly night
Vanish before His light.

When human hopes depart,
Draw closer to His heart.
His voice bids sorrow fly,
His love can satisfy;
His streams in deserts flow,
'Mid thorns His roses blow.

Then live, and do His work!
Let no repinings lurk
Within that heart which He
Loveth so faithfully.
Render Him love for love,
Like angel souls above.

Then, when the work is done,
The crown, the rest all won,
Not crown nor rest shall be
What most delighteth thee;
But gladness more divine, —
Thy Saviour, ever thine!

A. G. R.

WEDNESDAY.

TO Heaven I lift mine eye,
  To Heaven, Jehovah's throne,
For there my Saviour sits on high,
And thence shall strength and aid supply
  To all He calls His own.

He will not faint nor fail,
  Nor cause thy feet to stray;
For Him no weary hours assail,
Nor evening darkness spreads her veil
  O'er His eternal day.

Beneath that light divine
  Securely shalt thou move;
The sun with milder beams shall shine,
And eve's still queen her lamp incline
  Benignant from above.

For He, thy God and Friend,
Shall keep thy soul from harm,
In each sad scene of doubt attend,
And guide thy life, and bless thine end,
With His almighty arm.

JOHN BOWDLER.

EVEN to the end endure!
   In darkness as in light.
Clouds cannot make the stars less sure ;
   They only dim our sight.
Though sorrow reigns to-day,
   Joy in the morning waits ;
Fear not to tread the shadowed way
   To Heaven's golden gates.

Endure but to the end,
   Though doubts should fiercely rise!
The Lord shall from thy foes defend,
   And faith shall win the prize.
Thou hast a golden shield,
   And robes of spotless white —
Victory crowns thy battle-field ;
   Faith merges into sight!

6

Endure! the end will come;
 Endure! though fear would shake
The heart that yearns for rest and home
 As if that heart would break.
Danger and death may dare
 The soul that Heaven would win;
But oh, what glory waiteth there
 The vanquisher of sin.

Then to the end endure!
 Through darkness, doubt, and fear.
The fadeless morning standeth sure;
 Its roseate dawn is near.
Above the Cross I see
 The Crown's resplendent gleam;
Soon shall the bright Reality
 Eclipse earth's loveliest dream!

THEODOR CRUCIUS.

JESUS, help conquer!
    My spirit is sinking,
Deep waters of sorrow go over my head.
    Weeping and trembling,
    And fearing and shrinking,
I watch for the day, and night cometh instead.
    Bitter the cup
    I am hourly drinking —
How thorny the path that I hourly tread!

    Jesus, help conquer!
    For, fainting and weary,
Scarcely my hands can their weapons sustain.
    The way seems so desolate,
    Painful and dreary,
How shall I ever to Heaven attain?
    Jesus, Great Captain!
    If Thou be not near me,
How shall I ever the victory gain?

Jesus, help conquer!
Earth holds out her lure,
And mortal affections yearn after the prize
Scarcely my heart
Can the struggle endure;
Scarce can I lift up my tear-blinded eyes.
Jesus, Redeemer!
Thy promise is sure —
Speak to my spirit, and bid me arise.

Jesus, help conquer!
There is not an hour
Of sorrow or joy but is ordered by Thee:
Thou dost cut down
Who hast planted the flower —
Tempest or calm at Thy bidding shall be.
Look on my sorrow,
And give me the power
Humbly to wait till Thou comfortest me.

Jesus, help conquer!
I cry unto Thee!
Scarcely my heart its petitions can frame.
All is so dark

And so painful to me,
All I can utter sometimes is Thy name.
Jesus, help conquer !
My portion now be :
Though all else should change, be Thou ever
the same.

SCHRÖDER.

SATURDAY.

IN heavenly love abiding,
  No change my heart shall fear,
And safe is such confiding,
  For nothing changes here.
The storm may roar without me,
  My heart may low be laid,
But God is round about me,
  And can I be dismayed?

Wherever He may guide me,
  No want shall turn me back;
My Shepherd is beside me,
  And nothing can I lack.
His wisdom ever waketh,
  His sight is never dim;
He knows the way He taketh,
  And I will walk with Him.

Green pastures are before me,
  Which yet I have not seen ;
Bright skies will soon be o'er me
  Where the dark clouds have been.
My hope I cannot measure,
  My path to life is free,
My Saviour has my treasure,
  And He will walk with me.

A. L. WARING.

PALM SUNDAY.

THOU art worthy, Lord most holy!
    Endless praises to receive.
To our sin, our shame, and folly,
    Thou hast stooped, and bid us live.
Thou hast given us songs for sadness,
    Happy hearts for heaviness;
All Thy gifts to us are gladness,
    All Thy words breathe but to bless.

Lord of glory! all Thy splendor
    Hosts of Heaven but feebly sing!
But a song of thanks more tender,
    Lowlier, deeper, would we bring.
Seraphim must veil their faces:
    How could we Thy light endure,
If the love that thus abases
    Did not make the sinful pure?

Angels have their harps of glory,
  Innocent and joyful praise ;
We have but that one sweet story,
  Old as Calvary, to upraise.
We were lost, and Thou hast found us ;
  Thankless. yet Thy love was free ;
Wretched, till Thy pity crowned us ;
  Poor, but oh, how rich in Thee !

Oh how heartfelt, yet how lowly,
  Are the praises we should bring !
Lord most merciful, most holy !
  Thou art Heaven's majestic King.
Saints in ecstasy adore Thee,
  Thou of ecstasy the Source !
Sinners can but bow before Thee,
  Looking upward to Thy Cross.

A. G. R.

OVER against the city gates, in the flush
    of the eastern skies,
  The Lord, the King, looked down and wept
    for the day of mercy fled.
He saw the Temple's glittering front in the
    morning sunshine rise.
  He saw the shadows of doom loom up in
    the evening's lurid red.

O golden city of grace and peace, where
    shone God's altar-fires!
  Never shall prophet or priest sing out thy
    jubilee again.
Thy glory is dim, thy light is quenched in
    the passion of base desires;
  Thy King despised, rejected of men; thy
    Saviour smitten and slain.

Therefore that wailing voice rang out on the
    hushed, expectant air,

Therefore that vision of doom swept by
  when the hearts of the people slept;
Therefore, with bitter travail of soul, and the
  knell of a broken prayer,
The Lord looked over Jerusalem, and while
  He looked He wept.

My soul! has He never wept for thee? has
  His voice been never heard.
Pleading the things of eternal peace at thy
  heart's closed, frowning gate?
How often would He have gathered thee, hadst
  thou but by His love been stirred:
Oh, hear the call that is lingering yet;
  come forth ere it be too late!

Come forth, ere He leave thee, to meet thy
  King! not with the waving palm,
Not with the song of hosanna shouts that
  up through the sunshine rise;
But with the tears of a sorrowing heart, and
  a penitential psalm.
And eyes that are fixed on the lifted Cross
  where is slain thy Sacrifice.

Weep for the sins that have nailed Him there;
   for the record of long-past years,
For the folly and guilt of a thankless heart,
   for grace that was given in vain.
So shalt thou see like a rainbow rise, through
   the flood of those blinding tears,
The light of the love that illumes the world,
   and the pardon that heals thy pain.

Cling no more to thy pomp and pride; let
   thy heart's wild tumult cease;
Pray that thy soul may be pure from sin,
   and its old life fade away;
So shall He fold thee within His arms, and
   quiet thee into peace, —
So shall thy Passion with His o'erpass, and
   rise thine Easter-Day!

                                   A. G. R.

DEAR Lord! remember in that day
 Who was the cause Thou cam'st this way.
Thy sheep was strayed, and Thou wouldst be
Even lost Thyself in seeking me!

Shall all that labor, all that cost
Of love, and even that loss be lost?
And this loved soul judged worth no less
Than all that way and weariness?

Just mercy, then, Thy reckoning be
Made with my price, and not with me.
'T was paid at first with too much pain
To be paid twice, or once in vain.

Mercy, my Judge, mercy I cry,
With blushing cheek and bleeding eye.
The conscious colors of my sin
Are red without, and pale within.

O let Thine own compassion pay
Thyself, and so discharge that day!
If Sin can sigh, Love can forgive:
O say the word, my soul shall live!

Though both my prayers and tears combine,
Both worthless are, for they are mine:
But Thou Thy bounteous self still be,
And show Thou art by saving me.

R. CRASHAW.

OH ye who passe Me by, whose eyes and
  minde
To worldly things are sharp, but to Me blinde;
To Me who took eyes that I might you finde :
  Was ever grief like Mine ?

Judas, dost thou betray Me with a kisse ?
Canst thou finde hell about My lips ? and
  misse
Of life, just at the gates of life and blisse ?
  Was ever grief like Mine ?

All My disciples flie ; fear puts a barre
Betwixt My friends and Me. They leave the
  starre
That brought the Wise Men of the East from
  farre.
  Was ever grief like Mine ?

The priests and rulers all false witnesse seek
'Gainst Him who seeks not life, but is the
     meek
And readie Paschal Lambe of this great week.
    Was ever grief like Mine?

Upon My head a crown of thorns I wear;
For these are all the grapes Sion doth bear,
Though I My vine planted and watered there.
    Was ever grief like Mine?

Then with the reed they gave to me before,
They strike My head, the Rock from whence
     all store
Of heavenly blessings issue evermore.
    Was ever grief like Mine?

Yet since man's sceptres are as frail as reeds,
And thornie all their crowns, bloodie their
     weeds;
I, who am Truth, turn into truth their deeds.
    Was ever grief like Mine?

 The soldiers also spit upon that Face
Which angels did desire to have the grace,

And prophets once to see, but found no place.
    Was ever grief like Mine?

Shame tears My soul, My body many a wound;
Sharp nails pierce this, but sharper that con-
    found:
Reproaches which are free, while I am bound.
    Was ever grief like Mine?

Now heal thyself. Physician; now come down!
Alas! I did so, when I left My crown
And Father's smile for you, to feel His frown.
    Was ever grief like Mine?

Betwixt two thieves I spend My utmost breath,
As he that for some robberie suffereth.
Alas! what have I stolen from you?—death.
    Was ever grief like Mine?

They gave Me vinegar—mingled with gall,
But more with malice: yet, when they did call,
With manna, angels' food, I fed them all.
    Was ever grief like Mine?

Nay, after death their spite shall further go ;
For they will pierce My side, I full well know:
That as sinne came, so sacraments might flow.
    Was ever grief like Mine?

But now I die: now all is finishèd —
My woe, man's weal: so now I bow My head.
Only let others say when I am dead,
    Never was grief like Mine!

                    GEORGE HERBERT.

BREAD of the world, in mercy broken!
　　Wine of the soul, in mercy shed!
By whom the words of life were spoken,
　　And in whose death our sins are dead.

Look on the heart by sorrow broken,
　　Look on the tears by sinners. shed,
And be Thy feast to us the token,
　　That by Thy grace our souls are fed!

BISHOP HEBER.

THE blessed Cross shines now to us where
    once the Saviour bled;
Love made Him victim there for us, and there
    His blood was shed.

And with his wounds our wounds He healed,
    and washed our sins away,
And rescued from the raging wolf the lost and
    helpless prey.

There, with transfixèd palms, He hung, and
    saved the world from loss,
And closed the bitter way of death by dying
    on the Cross!

Those hands were pierced with cruel nails, fixed
    till His dying breath —
The hand that rescued Paul from crime, and
    Peter once from death!

O rich and fruitful branches! O sweet and no-
    ble Tree!
What new and precious fruit hangs for the world
    on thee ;

Whose fragrance breathes the breath of life into
    the silent dead —
Gives life to those from whom, long since,
    Earth's pleasant light had fled!

No summer heat has power to scorch who in
    thy shadow rest;
No moonlight chill can harm at night, no burn-
    ing noon molest.

Planted beside the water-flood, unshaken is thy
    root ;
Thy branch shall never fall nor fade, all sea-
    sons bear thy fruit.

For round thine arms entwining is the true and
    living Vine,
And from that blood-stained stem distils the
    new and heavenly wine!

V. FORTUNATUS.

BEHIND the silent tomb
Broods the dark night of gloom;
Beyond it, seas of light
Dazzle the straining sight;
Between, in beauty lies
The rest of Paradise.

There from the aching heart
Shall weariness depart;
There sorrow finds its balm,
Deep peace, bright, tireless calm.
Back in forgotten years
Lie trouble, toil, and tears.

Through that dark Gate of Death,
Parted by but a breath,
The Saviour bids us come.
And find with Him a home.
He is the Star to light
The shade of its calm night.

What bowers of amaranth bloom
Beyond that empty tomb,
What song of welcome swells
After earth's sad farewells,
Each for himself shall know —
But never here below !

As yet we only wait
Beside that dreadful Gate ;
Hear it swing to and fro,
As, one by one, we go ;
See sometimes through it gleam
Glories of which we dream.

So we say o'er and o'er,
" The Lord has gone before."
He knows which way is best ;
All paths lead to our rest.
Sunset of earthly skies
Is morn of Paradise !

A. G. R.

EASTER-DAY.

THE Day of Life is dawning! the Gate of
    Glory stands
Opened wide for the Conqueror — thronged
    by His angel bands.
The eastern skies are brilliant with a flood of
    crimson light,
The Morning bursts triumphant from the fet-
    ters of the Night;
And all creation's anthem joins the chorus from
    above,
" Christ has risen — He is risen! " 't is the fes-
    tal song of Love.

Oh what path of light leads upward from that
    silent, cheerless tomb!
From the crown of thorns what roses; round
    the Cross what lilies bloom!
What an arch of glory beameth o'er the chasms
    that divide

All the sorrows of the Passion from this ra-
diant Easter-tide !
Strange that clouds so long were shrouded
round that fair, life giving Sun !
But all darkness now is over, for the reign of
death is done.

So our Easter morning cometh, heralded by joy-
ful psalms ;
And we sing with white-robed angels, and we
wave the conquering palms ;
For the victory is ours, though not ours the
bloody strife :
By His pain our peace is purchased ; by His
death, our endless life.
But the Ransomer and ransomed shall together
rise and shine ;
His the Crown, our souls the jewels, and His
Cross the Throne divine.

See yon visitants descending from those cloudless morning skies, —
Faith, forever pointing upward ; Hope, with
. heavenward lifted eyes ;

Patience, with her staff of comfort; Love, with
    ardent, wistful gaze, —
Easter angels sent to guide us, in earth's few
    and evil days,
Through the tomb where once He slumbered,
    through all shadow and all sin,
To the Home where He is waiting, where with
    Him we enter in.

Wherefore then, O heart! be troubled? why, O
    trembling soul! cast down?
If to thee the Cross is given, He will give thee
    too the Crown.
Lo! the red dawn breaketh grandly o'er the
    battle-field of life!
What deep joy is born of sorrow! what sweet
    rest succeeds to strife!
For the eye that gazes upward sees no dim,
    uncertain ray —
Christ unveils all Heaven before us on this
    glorious Easter-Day.

Then to Him be thanks and honor. Sing aloud
    with heart and voice!

When the mighty Foe is fallen shall the con-
  querors not rejoice?
Pardon all our earthly discords, O benignant
  King of Saints!
Strengthen Thou our feeble praises, hush our
  faltering complaints!
Till with Angels and Archangels we shall mag-
  nify Thy grace,
, And shall rise, as Thou hast risen, to behold
  Thee face to face.

A. G R.

www.ingramcontent.com/pod-product-compliance
Lightning Source LLC
Chambersburg PA
CBHW032146010726
47493CB00008BA/2598